A WHOLE WORLD OF
MAMMALS

ANNA CLAYBOURNE AND YEKYUNG KWON

FRANKLIN
WATTS

First published in Great Britain in 2024 by Franklin Watts
Copyright © Hodder and Stoughton, 2024

Commissioning editor: Grace Glendinning
Designer: Lisa Peacock
Consultant: Dr Ashley Ward, professor of animal behaviour
at the University of Sydney

HB ISBN: 978 1 4451 8812 6
PB ISBN: 978 14451 8814 0
EB ISBN: 978 14451 8813 3

Printed and bound in Dubai

Franklin Watts, an imprint of
Hachette Children's Group
Part of Hodder and Stoughton
Carmelite House
50 Victoria Embankment
London EC4Y 0DZ
An Hachette UK Company

www.hachette.co.uk
www.hachettechildrens.co.uk

FSC
www.fsc.org

MIX
Paper | Supporting
responsible forestry
FSC® C104740

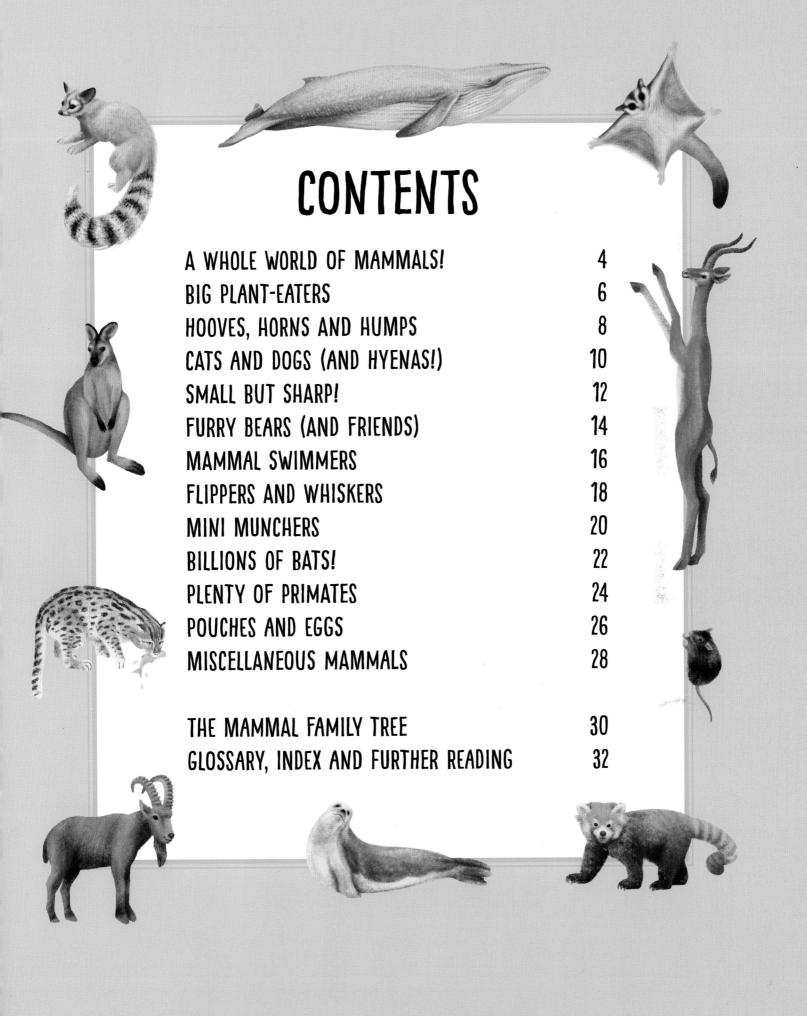

CONTENTS

A WHOLE WORLD OF MAMMALS!

Think of an animal ... and you'll probably think of a mammal. Cats, dogs, horses, dolphins, elephants, bears and monkeys – they're all mammals. And so are you!

WHAT ARE THEY?

Mammals come in many shapes and sizes, so what makes something a mammal?

- Mammals are warm-blooded – unlike a fish or a snake, they can warm up their own bodies from the inside, and usually have a warm temperature.

- They're often hairy or furry.

- They usually have four legs – or sometimes, two legs and two arms. Sea mammals have flippers.

- Mammals look after their babies, and mother mammals feed their babies with milk.

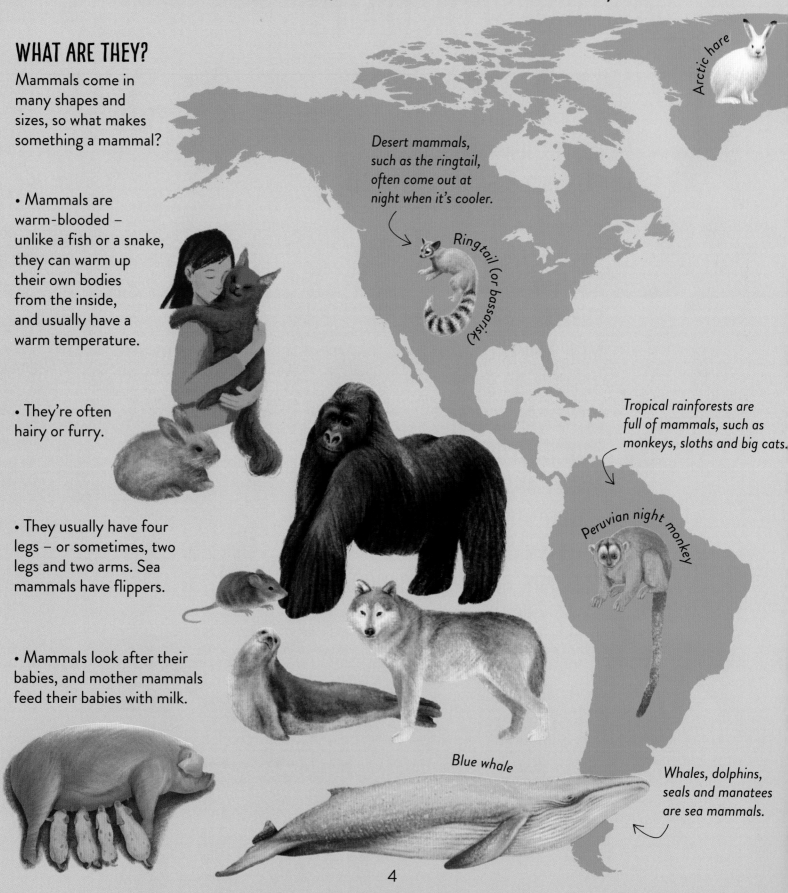

Arctic hare

Desert mammals, such as the ringtail, often come out at night when it's cooler.

Ringtail (or bassarisk)

Tropical rainforests are full of mammals, such as monkeys, sloths and big cats.

Peruvian night monkey

Blue whale

Whales, dolphins, seals and manatees are sea mammals.

MAMMAL MAP

The mammals are a huge family of animals, and they're found in almost every part of the world. Wherever they live, they are adapted, or suited, to their surroundings.

Polar bear

Extra-thick fur helps polar bears and Arctic hares survive the cold in the far north.

Shorthair cat

Some mammals live in our homes – like pet dogs and cats, or unwelcome mice or rats!

House mouse

Siberian ibex

The towering Himalayas are home to mountain ibexes and snow leopards.

All over the world, humans keep mammals as farm and working animals: examples include sheep, goats, cows, pigs, camels and horses.

Grevy's zebra

Zebras, lions, giraffes and gazelles roam the grassy savannah.

Domestic sheep

Verreaux's sifaka

Lemurs like this sifaka are only found on the island of Madagascar.

Wombat

HOW MANY MAMMALS?

There are about **6,400** different species, or types, of mammals. They're divided into different mammal groups, such as bears, bats, whales, wolves, apes and antelopes. To meet a ***whole world of mammals***, step this way!

5

BIG PLANT-EATERS

The big beasts you can see here are all plant-eaters, or herbivores.

WHY SO BIG?

Because when you're a plant-eater, it's easy to find lots of food and grow big. And, if you're big, it's harder for hunters to eat you. Being a monster-sized plant-muncher helps you survive.

ADAPTED TO SURVIVE

As in much of the natural world, these huge herbivores have evolved useful features to stay alive.

Giraffes' long necks help them feed on high-up tree leaves and branches.

Rhinos have horns for fighting and scaring away enemies.

Hippos' eyes, noses and ears are on the tops of their heads, so they can see and breathe as they swim in rivers, which are their natural habitat, or home.

African bush elephant

The African bush elephant is the biggest land animal. Males can be 7 m long and weigh 5,000 kg. That's about as much as 200 8-year-old humans!

Asian elephant

The other two elephant species are a bit smaller.

African forest elephant

Giraffe

Tallest animal in the world, at around 5 m in height.

White rhino

Critically endangered in the wild.

Indian rhino

Black rhino

Hippopotamus

African buffalo

These are two examples of wild cows …

American bison

FROM FARM TO FOREST

Cows and horses don't just live on farms! Both have tame and wild varieties.

Zebu

Highland cow

… while these four breeds are typically kept as farm animals.

Gaur

Ankole-Watusi

Shire horse

Two examples of domesticated horses:

Often found in showjumping and racing.

The biggest horse breed in the world.

Arab horse

Grevy's zebra

MORE MONSTER MAMMALS

Even elephants aren't the biggest mammals of all. Some are much more massive! You can find them on page 16.

Three members of the wild horse family:

Kiang

Przewalski's horse

HOOVES, HORNS AND HUMPS

Many plant-eating mammals are "ungulates", or mammals with hooves.

Moose, the biggest deer.

ANTLERS AND HORNS

Deer and antelopes are similar, but there's one big difference: what's on their heads!

Male deer (and female reindeer) have branching antlers.

Antelopes have horns instead of antlers, and female antelopes usually have them too.

Reindeer

Indian muntjac deer

The smallest antelope at just 25 cm high, the size of a cat!

Giant eland

The biggest antelope.

Blue wildebeest (or gnu)

Thompson's gazelle

Addax

Royal antelope

Antelope horns can be very long, and sometimes spiral-shaped.

Klipspringer

Can jump about 3 m high – five times their own height!

GRAZING AND NIBBLING

Goats are brilliant climbers and jumpers, and they nibble away at just about any plant.

Sheep graze on grass and have thick woolly coats.

Siberian ibex

Nubian Goat

Bharal

Merino sheep

Rocky Mountain goat

Also called blue sheep.

Kept for their extra-cosy wool.

8

THIS LITTLE PIGGY

Pigs come in lots of sizes, on the farm and in the wild!

Two varieties of wild pig:

Examples of domestic pigs

Warthog

Togian babirusa

Ibérico pig

Large white

Vietnamese pot-bellied pig

HOOVES IN THE JUNGLE

Related to horses and rhinos, tapirs are jungle ungulates.

Baird's tapir

Malayan tapir

Tapir babies, or calves, have spots and stripes to help them hide in the forest undergrowth.

Dromedary

Camel humps are made of stored fat.

Bactrian camel

Llamas are known for being social and hanging together in groups.

Alpaca

Llama

THE CAMEL FAMILY

These mammals are often kept for carrying heavy loads, or for their woolly hair. Camels come from Asia, but their smaller relatives are from South America.

Alpacas are famous for their soft wool.

9

CATS AND DOGS (AND HYENAS!)

Cats and dogs are carnivores, or meat-eaters. Both of these animal groups have species that have been domesticated to live among humans as pets.

Lion

BIG CATS

The tiger is the biggest cat, growing to 4 m long (including the tail). A large tiger can easily eat a human.

Tiger

Male lions have a large mane around their faces.

Leopard

A muscular, strong big cat with a very powerful bite.

Jaguar

Cheetah

The fastest cat – it can run at up to 120 km/h, as fast as a car on a motorway.

Ocelot

Tufty ears.

LITTLE CATS

These cats are closer to the size of a pet cat, or somewhere in between.

Caracal

Fishing cat

Scottish wildcat

Sand cat

Super fluffy!

Webbed feet for swimming and fishing in rivers and swamps.

Spotted hyena

WILD DOGS

These are the wild relatives of pet dogs.

Grey wolf

African hunting dog

Red fox

HYENAS

Hyenas are curious mammals that look a bit like dogs, but are more closely related to cats.

Enormous ears help it find and track down its prey.

Fennec fox

Dingo

Coyote

CUTE KITTIES AND BEST FRIENDS

Thousands of years ago, wild wolves and small wild cats began living alongside humans. In exchange for regular food and a safe home, the animals could catch pests or guard against enemies.

Today, many of us keep them in our homes to cuddle and pamper! Here is a selection of the breeds that humans have developed as pets over time.

Labrador retriever

DOMESTIC CATS

Border collie

Siamese

Maine coon

DOMESTIC DOGS

Bred for speed.

BIG and long-haired.

Greyhound

Bred for herding sheep.

Shorthair

No tail!

Manx cat

Chihuahua

Dachshund

SMALL BUT SHARP!

These mammals are not so big, but they are hunters just the same, and smart survivors.

Hedgehogs can curl up into a ball with their spines sticking out, to put off enemies.

Cuban solenodon

European hedgehog

Desert hedgehog

INSECT EATERS

Insectivores are mammals that hunt small prey, such as insects and worms. The very first mammals on Earth were mostly likely insect eaters!

Asian house shrew

Iberian desman

Moonrat

One of the world's smallest mammals – it's 4 cm long and weighs just 2 g, the same as a small coin.

Etruscan shrew

Caucasian mole

Tailless tenrec

(Not a real rat.)

This mammal has the most babies in a litter – up to 32!

Honey badger

BRAINY BADGER

The honey badger (or ratel) is sharp-clawed, fierce and incredibly clever. It has been known to use objects as tools to get itself out of tricky situations. And if that fails, its skin is very loose, so it's extra hard for a predator to grab on and keep hold.

WILY WEASELS

Weasels are small, cute, furry creatures. But did you know they have a wide range of weaselly relatives? All of these, from the stoat to the polecat, are part of the weasel family.

Mountain weasel

Stoat

Haida ermine

Eats rodents, birds and eggs, not fish!

Fisher

The biggest member of the weasel family.

European badger

Giant otter

Black-footed ferret

Pine marten

American mink

Marbled polecat

TOUGH COOKIES!

Mongooses and meerkats are famous for their ability to kill and eat dangerous creatures.

Indian grey mongoose

Meerkat

Meerkats make scorpions safe to eat by biting off their venomous stingers.

They can munch on snakes, as they are resistant to snake venom!

13

FURRY BEARS (AND FRIENDS)

Bears and bear-lookalike creatures have some fascinating traits and diets. Let's explore the true bears ... and those that are *not* true bears, despite very popular misconceptions!

BEWARE OF THE BEAR

Bears might remind you of your favourite stuffed toy, but don't get too close! They are deadly hunters, and some are VERY big.

Polar bear

American black bear

Asian black bear

Sun bear

Up to 3 m tall when it stands upright.

Spectacled bear

The clue's in the name and on its face!

Sloth bear

Ussuri brown bear of eastern Asia

The brown bear comes in the widest variety of types.

Syrian brown bear

Paler brown than the others.

Grizzly bear

Alaska's Kodiak bear

Hunts salmon.

Eurasian brown bear

PECULIAR PANDAS

The giant panda is an unusual type of bear. Even though it is classed as a carnivore, and its digestive system is well suited to meat, it mainly eats bamboo.

And the red panda is not related to the giant panda at all! It's more closely related to raccoons.

Red panda

Giant panda

Raccoon

Olinguito

Ringtail (or bassarisk)

Bearcat (or binturong)

MORE CUDDLY CREATURES

These are not true bears, but some assume they are, as they look similar, and some even have "bear" in their name.

Kinkajou

Wolverine

White-nosed coati or "nose bear".

They are very social and live in groups called bands or troupes.

Looks like a small bear, but it's a relative of weasels (see page 13).

MAMMAL SWIMMERS

Millions of years ago, some land mammals, related to today's hippos, evolved into sea creatures: the whales and dolphins, or cetaceans. They have no legs, and spend their whole lives in the water (though they can only breathe air).

MOUTH FILTERS

Baleen whales use their giant tongues to squeeze water out of their mouths through a sieve of baleen, trapping small sea creatures called krill.

Humpback whale

Sieve-like baleen

Blue whale

The blue whale is the biggest whale, mammal and animal in the world!

Whales and dolphins breathe through their blowholes. They're actually nostrils, but on top of their heads.

Bowhead whale

Sperm whale

Orca

WE'VE GOT TEETH!
Instead of baleen, the toothed whales, dolphins and porpoises have teeth. They mainly hunt fish, squid or seals.

Cuvier's beaked whale

Beluga whale

Indo-Pacific humpbacked dolphin

Common dolphin

Harbour porpoise

Bottlenose dolphin

Narwhal

The male's "horn" is an extra-long tooth.

RIVER DOLPHINS
A few unusual dolphins live in rivers in South America and Asia.

Amazon river dolphin

Ganges river dolphin

Indus river dolphin

The largest of the fresh water species.

Spinner dolphins spin around as they leap!

Spinner dolphin

Northern minke whale

Many whales and dolphins regularly breach, or leap out of the water.

FLIPPERS AND WHISKERS

These mammals are sea creatures, too, but some of them can climb out onto the land. And the sirenians are the slow-grazers of the sea ...

Southern elephant seal

The biggest seal – up to 5 m long.

Leopard seal

A fierce, penguin-eating Antarctic seal.

SO MANY SEALS!

Seals and sea lions have flippers instead of legs, which they use for swimming and for pushing themselves around on the seashore.

Ribbon seal

You can see how it got its name!

Crabeater seal

Seals use their whiskers to sense ripples underwater. This helps them to chase fish and find each other in the sea.

Grey seal

Harp seal

Weddell seal

Nerpa

These have cute, white, super-fluffy pups!

The only seal that lives in a lake instead of the sea – Lake Baikal in Russia, which is a long way inland, and no one knows how the nerpa got there.

18

SPOT THE EARS

Sea lions are nothing like lions! They're just a group of large seals with visible (but very small) ears. Fur seals have these ears, too.

Galapagos sea lion

Teeny ears!

Australian sea lion

California sea lion

Guadalupe fur seal

A very big relative of seals, with huge tusks up to 1 m long.

Walrus

Dugong

West African manatee

Amazonian manatee

MERFOLK OR CATTLE?

Sirenians are named after sirens, which is another name for mermaids. They're also known as "sea cows". Which do you think they look like most?

West Indian manatee

THE OTHER OTTERS

Most otters live in rivers, but the sea otter (and the marine otter in South America) prefer the ocean!

Sea otter

They float on their backs, using their stomachs as a dining table, or to carry their pups.

19

MINI MUNCHERS

Rodents and lagomorphs are known for being plentiful, but they are also enormously varied – in size, shape and habitat.

RODENTS – BEYOND THE BASEMENT

Most mice and rats live in the wild. Only a handful of species have adapted to live in human spaces.

House mouse

Delicate mouse

A very small wild mouse

Northern meadow jumping mouse

Striped grass mouse

Cactus mouse

Water rat

The biggest rat, as big as a cat!

Ferreira's spiny tree-rat

Brown rat

Black rat

Gambian pouched rat

SQUIRRELS, HAMSTERS, MARMOTS AND MORE

Like mice and rats, these rodent relatives all have long upper-middle teeth that grow constantly.

Big middle teeth.

Alpine marmot

Dormouse

Northern flying squirrel

Grey squirrel

Eastern chipmunk

European water vole

Mongolian gerbil

Scaly-tailed flying squirrel

Black agouti

Norway lemming

Muskrat

Chinese zokor

Nutria (or coypu)

Eurasian beaver

Domestic (pet) Guinea pig

Golden hamster

Mountain degu

Prairie dog

Common gundi

Chinchilla

Pygmy jerboa

Desert pocket gopher

Big back legs for hopping, like a kangaroo.

Famous for its extremely thick, soft fur.

Capybara

The biggest rodent! This species is the size of a large pig.

RABBITS, HARES AND PIKAS

Many people think rabbits and their relatives are rodents, but they are actually a separate family, the lagomorphs.

Amami rabbit

Angora rabbit

Volcano rabbit

Most lagomorphs have long, sticking-up ears.

Sumatran striped rabbit

Pygmy rabbit

Riverine rabbit

Arctic hare

European rabbit

Ili Pika

Pikas are small members of the rabbit family that live in high mountains.

Hainan hare

Tolai hare

Large-eared pika

BILLIONS OF BATS!

There are around 1,400 types of bat (more than a fifth of all mammal species!). They're also very numerous, as many species live together in huge colonies.

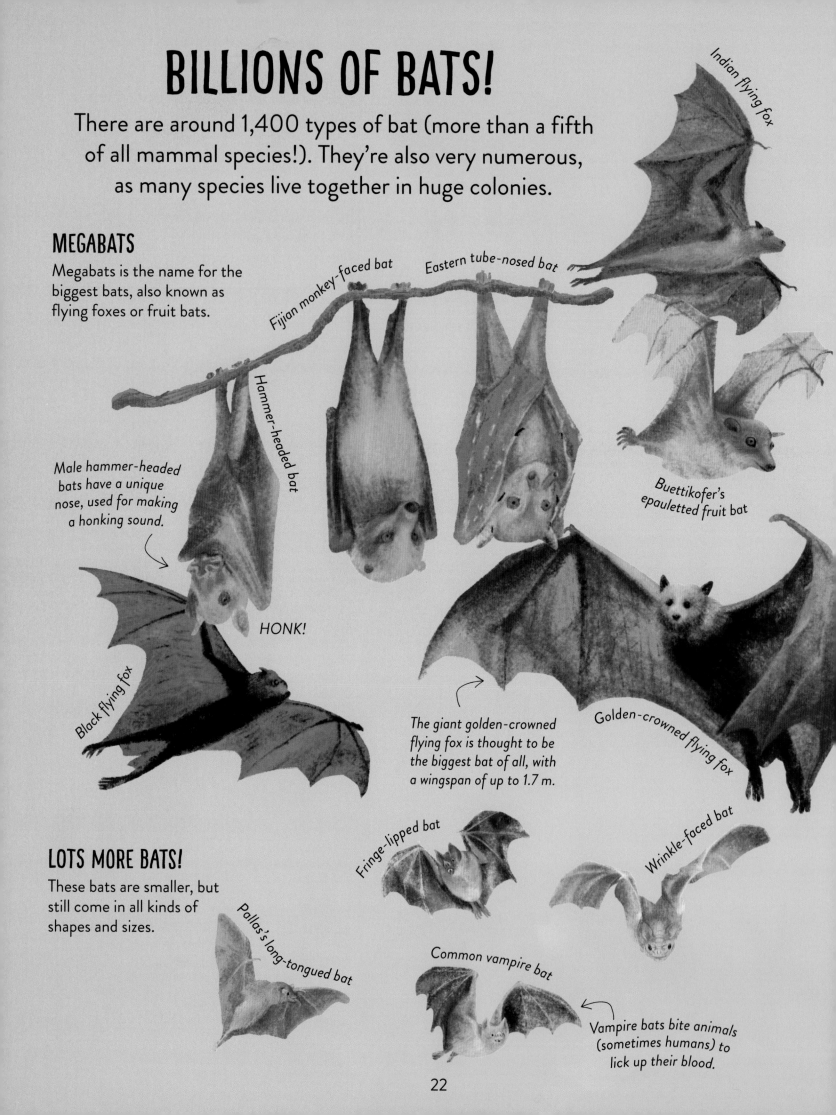

Indian flying fox

MEGABATS

Megabats is the name for the biggest bats, also known as flying foxes or fruit bats.

Fijian monkey-faced bat

Eastern tube-nosed bat

Hammer-headed bat

Male hammer-headed bats have a unique nose, used for making a honking sound.

Buettikofer's epauletted fruit bat

HONK!

Black flying fox

The giant golden-crowned flying fox is thought to be the biggest bat of all, with a wingspan of up to 1.7 m.

Golden-crowned flying fox

LOTS MORE BATS!

These bats are smaller, but still come in all kinds of shapes and sizes.

Fringe-lipped bat

Wrinkle-faced bat

Pallas's long-tongued bat

Common vampire bat

Vampire bats bite animals (sometimes humans) to lick up their blood.

Honduran white bat
(or tent-making bat)

In the daytime, these little bats snuggle up in a tent made out of a leaf.

Cuban funnel-eared bat

Pallid bat

New Zealand long-tailed bat

Kitti's hog-nosed bat
(or bumblebee bat)

Rufous horseshoe bat

SMALLEST OF ALL BATS:
only about 3 cm long.

Common pipistrelle

Common bent-wing bat

Egyptian tomb bat

Isabelle's ghost bat

Hoary bat

Rafinesque's big-eared bat

Mexican free-tailed bat

Madagascar sucker-footed bat

This species often lives in vast colonies of over a million bats.

Small mouse-tailed bat

Florida bonneted bat

Chapin's free-tailed bat

Greater bulldog or fisherman bat

Joffre's bat

Great evening bat

Swoooooops low over water to grab fish in its claws.

PLENTY OF PRIMATES

All of these mammals belong to a group called primates – from the biggest gorilla to the tiniest tarsier! We humans are primates, too.

Chimpanzee

Bonobo (or pygmy chimp)

APES
This group contains the largest primates.

Bornean white-bearded gibbon

Northern white-cheeked gibbon

Eastern gorilla

Lar gibbon

Gibbons' arms are longer than their legs!

Sumatran orangutan

The name orangutan means "person of the forest."

LEAPING LEMURS
These primates belong to their own unique family, found only on the large African island of Madagascar.

Hop and skip along the ground as if they're dancing!

Red ruffed lemur

Ring-tailed lemur

Verreaux's sifaka

Madame Berthe's mouse lemur

The smallest primate, at a teeny-weeny 9 cm long.

MONKEYS

Monkey species are divided into "New World" monkeys, from the Americas, and "Old World" monkeys, from Asia and Africa.

Hanuman langur

Check out its amazing nose!

Proboscis monkey

White-faced capuchin

Bald uakari

Mandrill

Golden snub-nosed monkey

NEW WORLD MONKEYS

Spider monkey

Peruvian night monkey

OLD WORLD MONKEYS

A nocturnal monkey.

Japanese macaque

Makassar tarsier

Bengal slow loris

Named for its call, which sounds like a baby crying in the night.

Mohol bushbaby

BIG-EYED CUTIE PIES!

Last but not least – say hello to the tarsiers and lorises. Both groups are known for their enormous eyes, which they use to hunt in the dark, as they are strictly nocturnal.

Silvery greater galago

Central African potto

25

POUCHES AND EGGS

Let's explore some really special mammal groups: marsupials and monotremes.

Marsupials give birth to very small babies, which cannot live away from their mum. They spend their first few months feeding on their mum's milk, usually living inside a warm, cosy pouch on her body.

FAMOUS MARSUPIALS

Probably the best-known and definitely the largest marsupial is the kangaroo.

Wallabies and wallaroos are close relatives of the kangaroo, and are just a bit smaller.

Red kangaroo

Antilopine kangaroo

Joey (baby) kangaroo in its mother's pouch.

Common wallaroo

Black wallaroo

Red-necked wallaby

Rufous hare-wallaby

Sugar glider

A sugar glider mum can even glide with babies in her pouch!

TINY POUCHES

There are tiny marsupials, too! Some scurrying on the ground, some climbing trees and some gliding through the air.

Quoll

Fat-tailed dunnart

Marsupial mole

Bilby

Numbat

Western grey kangaroo

The only opossum native to North America.

Virginia opossum

MOSTLY DOWN UNDER
Most marsupials are found in Australia and surrounding islands, with a few exceptions, such as the opossum.

Koala

Wombat

Some marsupials, including koalas, wombats and the Tasmanian devil, have pouches that face to the side or downwards.

Tasmanian devil

UNLIKE ANY OTHER
A few very unusual mammals, called monotremes, have babies by laying eggs. They include the duck-billed platypus and the echidna family.

Sir David's long-beaked echidna

Western long-beaked echidna

Platypus

Platypus eggs

Eastern long-beaked echidna

Short-beaked echidna

Echidnas are covered in quills and are also known as "spiny anteaters".

Platypuses live in rivers and have webbed feet for swimming.

27

MISCELLANEOUS MAMMALS

Some mammals are so unusual and unique, they need their own page!

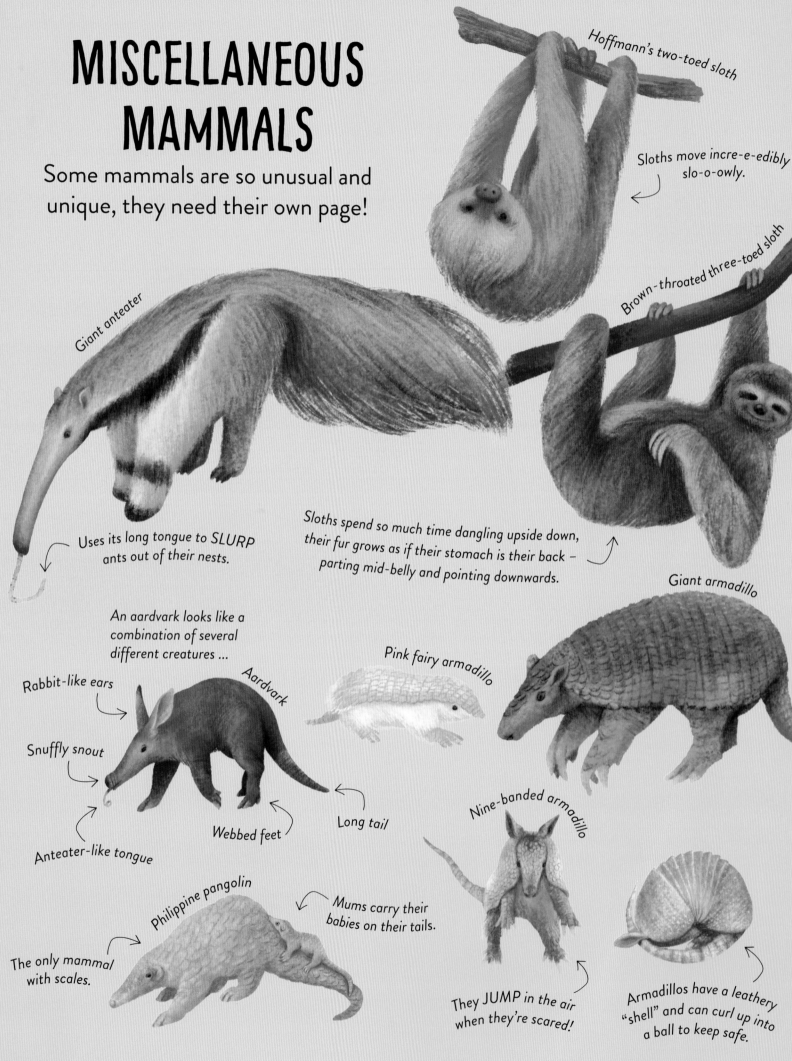

Hoffmann's two-toed sloth

Sloths move incre-e-edibly slo-o-owly.

Brown-throated three-toed sloth

Giant anteater

Uses its long tongue to SLURP ants out of their nests.

Sloths spend so much time dangling upside down, their fur grows as if their stomach is their back – parting mid-belly and pointing downwards.

Giant armadillo

An aardvark looks like a combination of several different creatures ...

Pink fairy armadillo

Rabbit-like ears

Aardvark

Snuffly snout

Long tail

Webbed feet

Anteater-like tongue

Nine-banded armadillo

Philippine pangolin

Mums carry their babies on their tails.

The only mammal with scales.

They JUMP in the air when they're scared!

Armadillos have a leathery "shell" and can curl up into a ball to keep safe.

28

Crested porcupine

Can run backwards to stick its long spines, or quills, into enemies!

Naked mole rat

Mostly hairless, pink, wrinkly, burrowing rodent.

Colugo

This primate has skin flaps connecting its limbs, which it uses to glide between trees.

Aye aye

Mini lemur with a very long, skinny finger for hooking insect larvae out of trees.

Star-nosed mole

22 tiny, touchy-feely nose "fingers"!

Chinese water deer

Fangs like a vampire!

Famous for spraying stinky liquid at enemies from its bum. Ewwwww!

Striped skunk

Bat-like ears!

Bat-eared fox

Gerenuk

Stands up like a human to reach tasty leaves.

THE ODDEST MAMMAL OF ALL

Humans

That's us!

We build complex technology and have big, complex brains.

We're the only mammals to wear clothes, cook with fire and read books!

29

THE MAMMAL FAMILY TREE

Here are all the main mammal groups at a glance.
This family tree shows you how they're all related,
with similar types sharing the same main branches.

Can you find your favourites?

Seals and
sea lions

Giraffes

Antelopes

Pangolins

Cats

Deer

Hyenas

Camels

Sheep

Cows

Hippos

Pigs

Bats

Whales and
dolphins

MARSUPIALS

MONOTREMES

MAMMAL

30

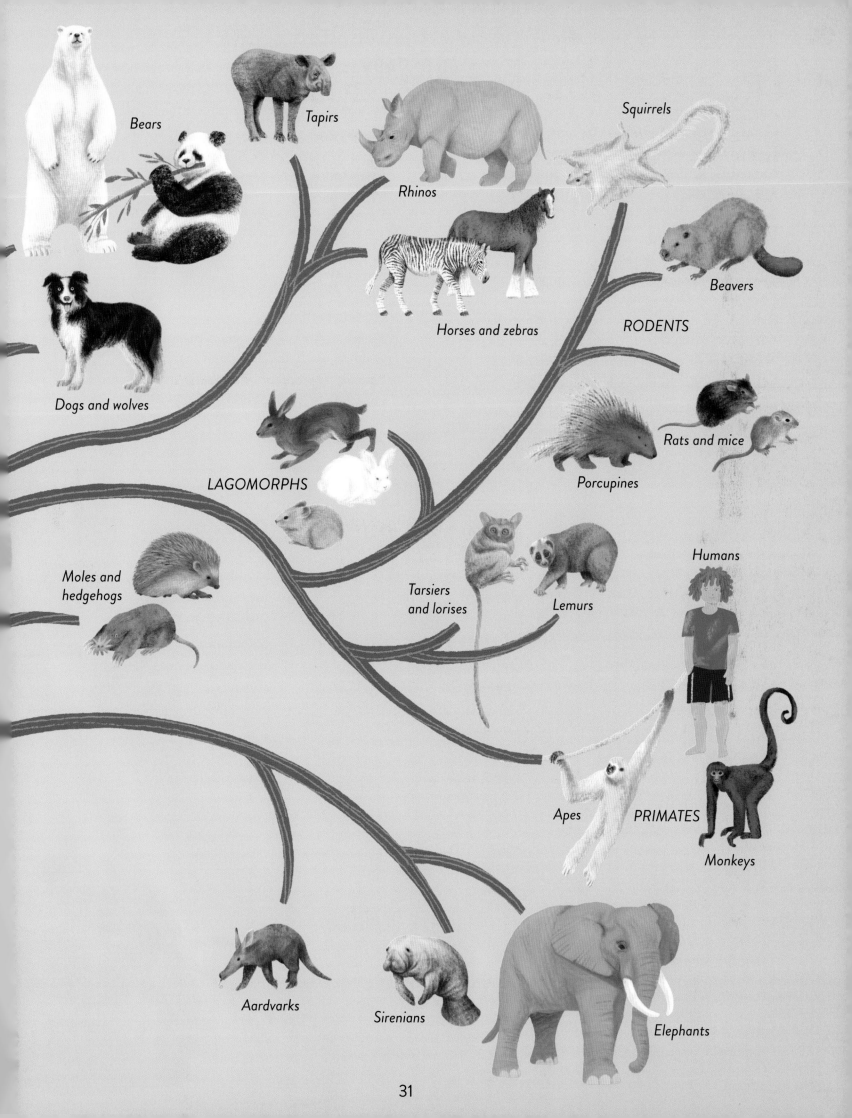

Bears

Tapirs

Squirrels

Rhinos

Horses and zebras

RODENTS

Beavers

Dogs and wolves

LAGOMORPHS

Porcupines

Rats and mice

Moles and hedgehogs

Tarsiers and lorises

Lemurs

Humans

Apes

PRIMATES

Monkeys

Aardvarks

Sirenians

Elephants

31

GLOSSARY

Adaptation A process by which living things gradually change over time to suit the surroundings or conditions.

Carnivore An animal that eats other animals.

Cetaceans Whales, dolphins and porpoises.

Colony A group of animals, such as bats, that live together.

Domestic animal An animal bred to be tame, and used as a farm animal or pet.

Evolution A process of gradual change over many generations of living things.

Extinct An extinct species is one that has died out and no longer exists.

Herbivore An animal that eats plants.

Insectivore An animal that feeds on insects and other small animals.

Lagomorph A type of small furry mammal, including rabbits and hares.

Mammal A type of animal that feeds its babies on milk.

Marsupial A type of mammal that carries it babies in a pouch on the mother's underside.

Monotreme A rare type of mammal that has babies by laying eggs.

Pinniped A type of water mammal with flippers, such as a seal or sealion.

Primate A type of mammal with forward-facing eyes and human-like hands, including monkeys and apes.

Rodent A type of smallish mammal with constantly growing teeth.

Sirenian A type of large sea mammal that feeds on seagrass, such as a dugong or manatee.

Species A group of living things that are very similar.

Ungulate An animal with hooves.

INDEX

FURTHER READING

There Are Mammals Everywhere
By Camilla de la Bedoyere and Britta Teckentrup (Big Picture Press, 2022)

Ultimate Explorer Field Guide: Mammals
(National Geographic Kids, 2019)